PUFFIN BOOKS

D0009318

PIRATE PENGUINS

Frank Rodgers has written and illustrated a wide range of books for children – picture books, story books, non-fiction and novels. His children's stories have been broadcast on radio and TV and he created a sitcom series for CBBC based on his book *The Intergalactic Kitchen*. His recent work for Puffin includes the Eyetooth books and the bestselling Witch's Dog and Robodog titles. He was an art teacher before becoming an author and illustrator and lives in Glasgow with his wife. He has two grown-up children.

Frank Rodgers
Pirate
Penguins

PUFFIN

For penguins everywhere. Happy fishing.

PUFFIN BOOKS

Published by the Penguin Group
Penguin Books Ltd, 80 Strand, London WC2R 0RL, England
Penguin Group (USA) Inc., 375 Hudson Street, New York, New York 10014, USA
Penguin Group (Canada), 90 Eglinton Avenue East, Suite 700, Toronto, Ontario, Canada M4P 2Y3
(a division of Pearson Penguin Canada Inc.)
Penguin Ireland, 25 St Stephen's Green, Dublin 2, Ireland (a division of Penguin Books Ltd)
Penguin Group (Australia), 250 Camberwell Road, Camberwell, Victoria 3124, Australia
(a division of Pearson Australia Group Pty Ltd)
Penguin Books India Pvt Ltd, 11 Community Centre, Panchsheel Park,
New Delhi – 110 017, India
Penguin Group (NZ), cnr Airborne and Rosedale Roads, Albany, Auckland 1310, New Zealand
(a division of Pearson New Zealand Ltd)
Penguin Books (South Africa) (Pty) Ltd, 24 Sturdee Avenue, Rosebank,
Johannesburg 2196, South Africa

Penguin Books Ltd, Registered Offices: 80 Strand, London WC2R 0RL, England

www.penguin.com

First published 2006
1
Text and illustrations copyright © Frank Rodgers, 2006

The moral right of the author/illustrator has been asserted

Set in MT Times New Roman Schoolbook
Printed in China by Midas Printing Ltd

British Library Cataloguing in Publication Data
A CIP catalogue record for this book is available from the British Library

ISBN-13: 978–0–141–31826–4
ISBN-10: 0–141–31826–0

Chapter One

"I do love the pirate life," cried Paisley from the deck of his iceberg ship, the *Frozen Kipper*. "Sailing the seas, chasing treasure, being a big, bad, bold buccaneer . . ."

"Having lunch," added Posso, the
first mate.

"What's that got to do with being a
pirate?" asked Paisley.
"Nothing," replied Posso. "It's just
that I'm hungry."

Paisley grinned.
"So am I," he
said. "What's for
lunch, Kelty?"

Kelty, the cook, looked up from
behind the galley stove.

"Nothing, I'm
afraid," he said.
"We ate everything
at breakfast."

Just then Spott, the
lookout, shouted,
"Ship ahoy! The
Flying Walrus."

"A ship! Just
what we need,"
said Paisley.
"We'll get some lunch the pirate
way."

4

The *Frozen Kipper* set off in pursuit.

Scudding across the waves, the big
lump of ice soon caught up with the
Flying Walrus.

Paisley leapt aboard, waving his cutlass.

"Ahar!" he cried at the startled sailors. "It is I . . . the pirate penguin. Hand over your fish!"

"Sorry," said the sailors. "We
haven't caught any today.

All we have are ship's biscuits and
dried peas. Oh, and treasure, of
course."

Paisley frowned.
"Ship's biscuits and
dried peas are no
good to penguins," he
said. "And we've got
enough treasure."
Shaking his head in
disappointment he
clambered back
aboard the
Frozen Kipper.

But as they sailed away Spott called
out again from the crow's nest.
"Ship ahoy! The *Singing Squid*."

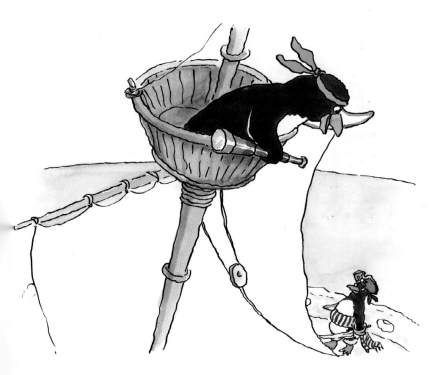

"Aha," cried Paisley. "Maybe we'll
have better luck this time."

Once more the *Frozen Kipper* set sail
and sped across the sea. As they
reached the *Singing Squid* Paisley
leapt aboard, waving his cutlass.

"It is I . . . the dreaded pirate
penguin. Hand over your fish!"

But once more the reply was the same.

"Sorry. We haven't caught any today. All we have are ship's biscuits and dried peas. Oh, and treasure, of course."

"There's nothing for it," said Paisley as the *Frozen Kipper* sailed away. "We'll just have to catch some fish ourselves."

Chapter Two

All that day Paisley and his crew fished in the wide, blue ocean.

But by the time evening came they hadn't caught a single thing.

"We must be the worst fish-catchers
in the world!" exclaimed Paisley.
"A budgie with a
blindfold could
do better."

"Ship ahoy!" yelled Spott for the
third time. "The *Juicy Bone.*"

Paisley looked up and saw a
brightly painted fishing boat off the
port bow.

At its helm was
a whiskery
old sea dog.

"A fishing boat!" shouted Paisley.
"*Exactly* what we need."

The *Frozen Kipper* quickly came alongside the *Juicy Bone* and Paisley jumped aboard, a big grin on his face.

"It is I . . . the pirate penguin!" he cried, waving his cutlass. "Hand over your fish!"

Dunoon, the old sea dog, sighed and scratched his whiskers.

"Wish I could, matey," he said. "But there's not a fish left in the sea. I've looked. They've all gone."

Paisley's face fell. "So that's why we couldn't catch any," he said.

"That's why," said Dunoon.

"But where have the
fish gone?" asked
Paisley. "Do you
know?"

"I do," replied
the old sea dog.
"I do. The cats
took them."

"The cats? What
cats?" asked
Paisley, puzzled.

"The cats in their big ships with
their big nets," answered Dunoon.

"They came and swept the sea clean.
Took everything from tiddlers to
tuna, from sardines to swordfish.
Emptied the ocean, they did."

"But what about the rest of us?"
called Posso from the *Frozen Kipper*.
"What are we going to eat?"

"The cats don't care,"
said Dunoon.

"But that's so selfish!" gasped
Paisley.

"I know," replied the old sea dog. "If you want to do something about it you could go to Octopus Island.

That's where the cats are. But be careful. They're fearsome."

"Don't worry about us," said Paisley confidently. "We're pirates . . . big, bad, bold buccaneers."

Chapter Three

The *Frozen Kipper* reached
Octopus Island that night under
a bright, full, yellow moon.

"This place is supposed to be
haunted by the ghost of a giant
octopus," said Posso nervously as
they crept up the beach.

"Nonsense," said Paisley. "Nothing
to be afraid of. Remember, we're
big, bad, bold . . ."

MEEAAAOOOW!

A horrible shriek suddenly cut
through the night air and froze them
in their tracks.

Before they knew what was
happening they were surrounded by
cats – enormous, furry, sharp-toothed
cats.

"Oh, yessss," hissed their captain.
"Penguins. Lovely! A nice change
from fish. We'll have them for
breakfast in the morning."

He pointed up the hill with a
wicked-looking claw. "Take them to
the jail."

The bloodthirsty cats marched their prisoners to the top of the hill.

From the top Paisley could see the cats' harbour town spread out below in the moonlight.
He gasped.

The two harbour walls stretched out
like giant stone arms. Between them
the sea was crammed full . . . of
fish!

The fish were kept in by big, iron
gates across the harbour entrance. It
was like a huge, fishy prison – the
world's biggest sardine can.

Paisley and his crew didn't have
much time to look.
"Get a move on, breakfasts!" cried
the cats, snorting with laughter.

They pushed and prodded the pirate
penguins down to the town – and
straight into the jail.

"Now what are we going to do?"
moaned Posso as the door was
locked behind them.

"We're doomed! We're cats'
breakfasts now!"

"Yes," Spott chimed in. "We found the fish all right . . . but only after the cats found *us*!" Everyone turned to Paisley.

"What are we going to do?"

Paisley folded his flippers.
"Give me a moment," he said.
"I'll think of
something. I
usually do."
The crew
waited . . .
and waited
. . . and
waited.

Chapter Four

Two hours later Paisley still hadn't thought of anything. He tapped a webbed foot impatiently on the floor and thought some more. Suddenly he looked down to where he had been tapping.

"This floor is sandy," he said. "Perhaps we could dig ourselves out!"

"Worth a try," replied Posso. "We've got strong beaks and flippers."

So they set to work.

To cover the noise of Paisley and
Posso digging, Spott and Kelty sang
an old sea-shanty.

"Blow the cat down,
penguins, blow the
cat down . . .

Yo, ho! Blow
the cat down."

"What a racket," complained the
guards. "It's even worse than a cats'
chorus!"

But the two penguins
kept singing . . .

. . . and Paisley and Posso kept
digging the tunnel.

At last, hot and dusty, Paisley and
Posso wriggled through and emerged
behind the jail.

But just as Spott and Kelty were
about to join them there was a strange
rumbling sound underground . . .

. . . and the tunnel caved in.
"Oh, no!" gasped Kelty and Spott,
jumping back just in time.
"We're stuck in
here and it'll
be morning
soon.

No time to dig another tunnel."

"Don't worry," Paisley whispered to
them through the barred window.

"We'll come
back and rescue
you."

"How will we do that?" asked Posso
softly as they crept away.

"Ah," said Paisley. "I have a plan. Not only will we save Spott and Kelty, but we'll get rid of the cats and free the fish at the same time."

"But how?" whispered Posso again.

"Follow me," replied Paisley. "You'll see."

They carefully sneaked past all the
guards until they made it safely
back to the beach.

With their flippers hardly making a
sound in the water they paddled
their small slab of ice out to the
Frozen Kipper.

Once they were aboard Paisley
gazed down into the hold.

"Right, Posso," he
said. "Let's bring
up the spare set
of sails."

Posso looked puzzled but just
shrugged his shoulders.
"If you say so," he said.

A few minutes later the big white
sails were laid on the deck.

Paisley appeared from his cabin a
moment later with scissors, needle,
thread, paint and brushes.

"Now," he whispered, "this is what
we're going to do."

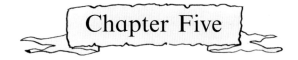

Chapter Five

I t was still dark but morning
wasn't far off.
The cats were getting hungry.

"How do you like your penguins?"
asked the cats' captain.
"Boiled," said the first mate.

"Scrambled," replied
the lookout.

"Fried,"
answered the
cook.

The captain grinned and licked his
lips.
"I'm rather fond
of penguin
sausages myself,"
he said.

Just then the first mate happened to
look up into the night sky and
jumped with fright.
"Wh . . . what's that?" he stammered,
pointing.

Out of the darkness
loomed a huge, ghostly white shape.
It drifted towards them slowly on
the sea breeze.

"It . . . it's an enormous octopus!"
gasped the captain. He stared at the
horrible object with its eight tentacles
waving in the wind.
"The . . . the ghost
of Octopus Island!"

"I told you this place was haunted!"
yelped the cook.

The giant octopus suddenly gave a
ghostly howl.

"I *am* the ghost of
Octopus Island!"
it wailed. "And
you have stolen
all my fish! I
have come for
revenge."

OOOOOOW!

"Aaaaagh!" shrieked the cats.
"We're sorry! We won't do it again.
Honest. Look . . . we're leaving."

The cats rushed down to the harbour
and opened the iron gates.

As the fish swam free the frightened
felines jumped into their ships and
sailed away as fast as they could.
They were never seen again.

The ghostly octopus slowly drifted
over the town and landed in front of
the jailhouse.
Paisley and Posso got out of the
basket which was hidden underneath.

"What a brilliant idea of yours to sew the sails together and make a balloon," said Posso. "And to fill it up with hot air from the galley chimney."

Paisley grinned. "Just as well you knew that this place was supposed to be haunted," he replied.

Quickly the two pirate penguins
unlocked the jailhouse door.

"Hooray for Paisley and Posso!"
exclaimed Spott and Kelty, delighted
to be set free.

Posso grinned.
"Thanks," he said.
"Now . . . let's go and
get some breakfast."

"Yes . . . but let's do it the pirate
way!" cried Paisley. "We're big, bad,
bold buccaneers so we'll board the
first ship we see and I'll shout . . ."

Hand over your fish!

Chapter Six

Hurrying over the hill and down to the beach, Paisley and his crew paddled out to the *Frozen Kipper*.

But when they climbed aboard they got a surprise. On the middle of the deck stood a big basketful of fish.

Attached to the basket was a note.
"I saw what you did and caught
these for you," it said.

"Thank you for your good deed.
Now there's plenty of fish for
everyone again." It was signed
"Captain Dunoon of the *Juicy
Bone*."

"That's so nice," said Paisley,
smiling. Then he frowned.
"But pirates aren't supposed to do
good deeds."

He looked at the fish hungrily.
"Never mind, though," he said.
"Let's tuck in."

When everyone had eaten their fill
they sat contentedly on the deck.
The *Frozen Kipper* rocked gently on
the blue waves under the morning
sun.

Suddenly Spott
sat up.
"What's that
noise?" he said.
Everyone listened and heard a *plip-
plop* sound.

"Something's dripping," said Kelty.
Paisley splashed his flipper in a
nearby puddle.

"Oh, oh," he
cried, jumping
up. "It's us! The
ship's melting!
Come on . . . I
think we'd better
go home."

The crew rushed about setting
the sails and the big lump of ice
slowly turned round and headed
north again.